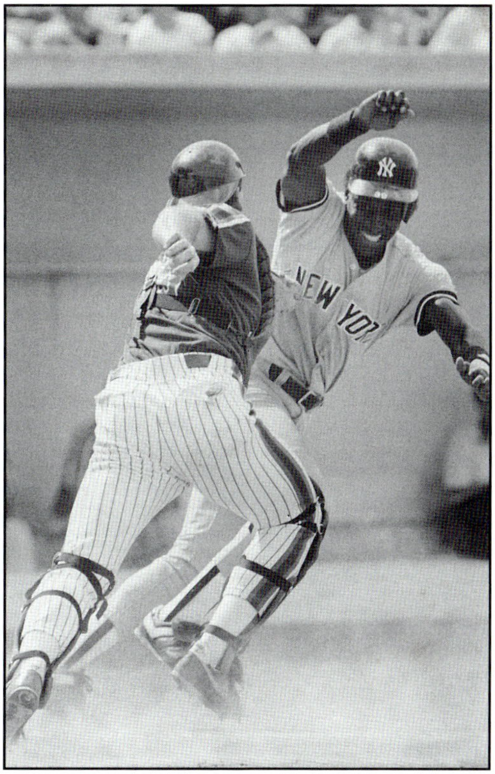

CREATIVE EDUCATION

AL EAST

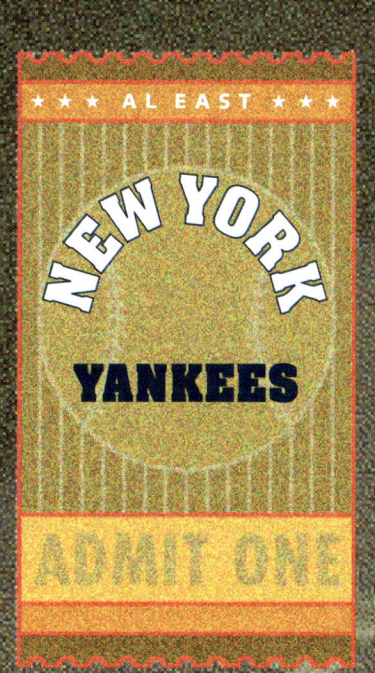

NEW YORK YANKEES

ADMIT ONE

RICHARD RAMBECK

Published by Creative Education, Inc.
123 S. Broad Street, Mankato, Minnesota 56001

Art Director, Rita Marshall
Cover and title page design by Virginia Evans
Cover and title page illustration by Rob Day
Type set by FinalCopy Electronic Publishing
Book design by Rita Marshall

Photos by Allsport, Duomo, Focus on Sports,
FPG, National Baseball Library, Michael Ponzini,
Sports Illustrated, Superstock, UPI/Bettmann,
Ron Vesley and Wide World Photos

Copyright © 1992 Creative Education, Inc.
International copyrights reserved in all countries.
No part of this book may be reproduced in any form
without written permission from the publisher.
Printed in the United States of America.

Library of Congress Cataloging-in-Publication Data

Rambeck, Richard.
  New York Yankees / by Richard Rambeck.
    p. cm.
  Summary: A team history of the most successful professional team in the history of U.S. sports.
    ISBN 0-88682-445-1
  1. New York Yankees (Baseball team)—History—Juvenile literature. [1. New York Yankees (Baseball team)—History. 2. Baseball—History.] I. Title.
GV875.N4R19 1991   91-2477
796.357'64'097471—dc20   CIP

THE EARLY YEARS

Known as the "Big Apple," New York City has more than twice the population of any other U.S. metropolis. Located in the southeastern corner of the state of the same name, New York is one of the largest centers of commerce in the world. The city has been the hub of U.S. economic activity for more than two centuries.

New York's importance in American business becomes obvious when one looks at the city's skyline. Huge buildings tower over the city's downtown core. They are home to the many businesses that are headquartered in New York. These structures include the Empire State Building and the World Trade Center. Buildings along Wall Street house the nation's largest stock exchanges.

"The House That Ruth Built," Yankee Stadium.

The Highlanders finished fourth in their first year in the AL under the guidance of manager Clark Griffith.

But New York isn't all business. The largest city in the United States also has a grand sports tradition, one that includes the most successful professional team in the history of U.S. sports—the New York Yankees of major-league baseball. No American professional team has won as many championships as the Yankees, who have claimed twenty-two World Series titles. The team has also won an unbelievable thirty-four American League pennants. In addition, the New York club is the only major-league team in history to win five World Series in a row (1949–53) and the only squad to win four consecutive titles (1936–39).

The Yankees' story is not only loaded with successful seasons, it is also filled with the exploits of superstars, players who are some of the best-known in the game's history. Babe Ruth was perhaps the greatest home-run hitter of all time. Lou Gehrig was probably the most durable athlete in the history of American sports. Joe DiMaggio and Mickey Mantle were dynamic and multi-talented center fielders. Reggie Jackson was a slugger with an incredible sense of making the most of a big moment. And Don Mattingly might be the most consistent hitter in the game today. Amazingly, these players represent only a fraction of the many great talents who have played for New York over the years.

Despite their glorious history, the Yankees were not successful during the early years of the franchise. The club became a member of the American League in 1903 and was then known as the Highlanders. The Highlanders were rarely high in the league standings: they seldom finished above fourth in the eight-team American League during the first fifteen years of the

Another Yankee great, Steve Sax.

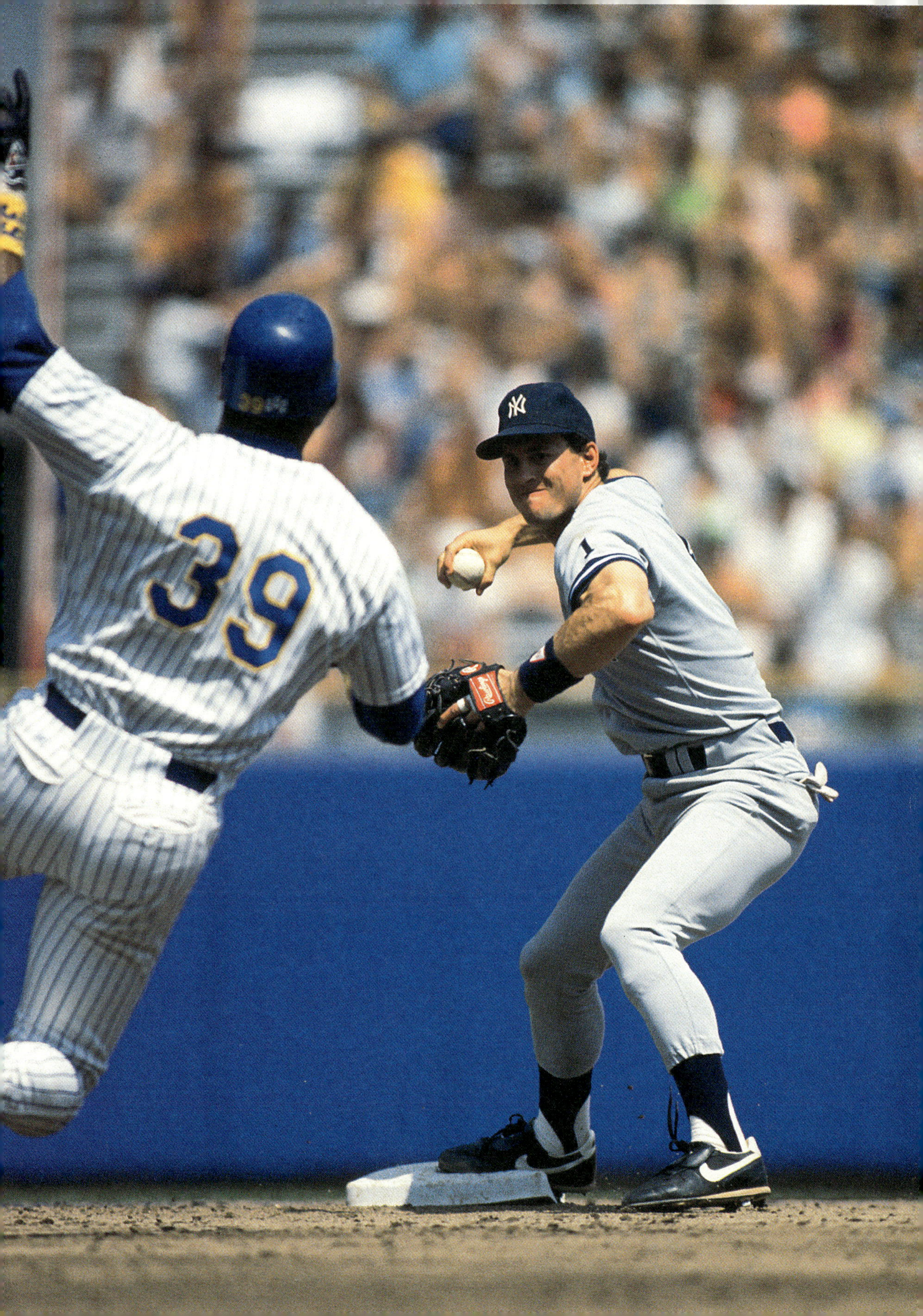
39

On April 15, pinstripes, now a Yankee tradition, first appeared on the club's uniforms.

franchise. The team, which was also called the Hilltoppers and finally the Yankees, was only the third most popular club in New York City, behind the New York Giants and the Brooklyn Dodgers of the National League, which were much more successful. Finally, in 1918, tired of the Yankees being the "other" team in the Big Apple, the Yankee owners persuaded Miller Huggins, the feisty little manager of the St. Louis Cardinals, to accept a new position as manager of the New York team.

RUTH AND GEHRIG POWER THE YANKS TO THE TOP

Huggins decided to build his team on power hitting, and his first club, in 1919, led the American League in home runs with forty-five, thanks mostly to slugging outfielder Duffy Lewis. That same year, however, one player for the Boston Red Sox hit twenty-nine homers all by himself. That player's name was George Herman Ruth, better known as the "Babe." Huggins begged management to go after Ruth, and the Yankees did just that, trading for Ruth and then offering him a contract with a salary four or five times larger than most major-league salaries at the time. Ruth, who began his career as a pitcher for the Red Sox but who had become a full-time right fielder, joined the Yankees in time for the 1920 season. Three years later the Yankees, now among the top teams in baseball, added another slugger, a first baseman who would bat cleanup behind the amazing Ruth. The new power hitter, a six-foot, two-hundred-pounder from Columbia University in New York City, was named Lou Gehrig. Ruth and Gehrig were the major stars in a lineup that would eventually be called

Murderers' Row. Behind the hitting of Ruth and Gehrig, the Yankees won four World Series titles and five American League pennants between 1923 and 1932. In all, Ruth, who left the Yankees in the mid-1930s, played on seven pennant winners; Gehrig, whose career ended in 1939, was a member of nine American League championship teams and eight World Series winners.

Ruth and Gehrig had a lot in common on the field—both were power hitters who had high batting averages—but they were as different as night and day off the diamond. Ruth was a playful sort, a little boy who never grew up; Gehrig, who had much more formal education than Ruth, was serious and shy. In truth the two superstars respected each other much more than they liked each other.

Ruth, who was always acting up as a child, never stopped having a good time during his baseball career. One Yankee player who was assigned to share a hotel room with Ruth on road trips said that he shared the room with "Babe Ruth's suitcase," because Ruth was never there.

Ruth was known for his late-night antics, but he also had a soft spot in his heart for kids. He made numerous visits to the children's wards at New York hospitals. He also would stand for hours signing autographs.

Ruth was revered by the kids, and he was respected by his teammates, many of whom were in awe of his talents. Said Waite Hoyt, who was Ruth's teammate with the Yankees from 1921 to 1930: "To play on the same club with Ruth was not only a pleasure, it was a privilege—an experience which comes once in a life-time. Babe was no ordinary man. He was superman to

Two historic events occurred on April 18: Yankee Stadium opened and Babe Ruth hit the first home run.

Continuing the tradition of Ruth and Gehrig, Kevin Maas.

The next Yankee Hall of Famer, Rickey Henderson.

1 9 2 7

"The Sultan of Swat," Babe Ruth (right), led the AL in both home runs and RBI.

the ballplayers. Ballplayers who had played against him and who eventually joined the Yankees used to say, 'I knew how great he was when I played against him, but I never thought I'd see anything like this.'"

Ruth, who retired with a .342 lifetime batting average, hit 714 regular-season home runs during his remarkable career. He also hit fifteen homers during World Series play. Ruth topped the American League in home runs twelve times. In 1927 Ruth slammed sixty homers, a single-season record that stood until Roger Maris, another Yankee slugger, hit sixty-one in 1961. Ruth, perhaps the most feared power hitter of all time, managed to hit one home run approximately every twelve times at bat. He was so famous that sportswriters began calling Yankee Stadium, which the team moved into during Ruth's early years with the club, the "House That Ruth Built."

If Ruth was spectacular, Gehrig was steady. Ruth was known for towering, tape-measure blasts; Gehrig was more of a line-drive hitter. "He could probably hit a ball harder in every direction than any man who ever played," said Yankee pitcher Bill Dickey of Gehrig. "Lou could hit hard line drives past an outfielder the way I hit hard line drives past an infielder."

When Gehrig joined the Yankees in 1923, he initially sat on the bench. Veteran Wally Pipp was a standout at first base. Despite this, manager Miller Huggins was determined to use Gehrig somehow, and Huggins got his chance when Pipp complained of a headache one day and asked to be taken out of the lineup. Gehrig started at first base, and remained there for 2,130 consecutive games, an all-time major-league record that may never be broken. Today, almost sixty years after Gehrig made his Yankee debut, sportswriters still refer to the "Wally Pipp disease" anytime a starter, in any sport, sits out a game or two and is replaced by a substitute who does well. In the case of Gehrig, Pipp's headache cost him any chance of ever regaining his starting spot with the Yankees.

Because Gehrig never came out of the lineup, most fans thought he was indestructible. In fact, Gehrig was given the nickname "Iron Horse" because of his durability. But he wasn't indestructible. By the beginning of the 1939 season, it was obvious that Gehrig wasn't himself. He was sluggish, and he couldn't seem to hit at all. What nobody knew at the time was that the mighty Lou Gehrig was dying. Gehrig had come down with an incurable disease known as amyotrophic lateral sclerosis, which destroys the nerve cells that control movement. Doctors told Gehrig there was no hope, but he refused

The Yankees finished second in Joe McCarthy's first of fifteen full seasons as New York manager.

On June 2, at the age of 37, Yankee great Lou Gehrig died.

to believe it. The illness forced him to retire during the 1939 season. On July 4 of that year, the Yankees held "Lou Gehrig Day" at Yankee Stadium. Before the game an obviously weakened Gehrig walked slowly to the microphone and, with the crowd's cheers almost drowning him out, said, "Today, I consider myself the luckiest man on the face of the earth." Two years later the Iron Horse was dead at age thirty-eight. Today, fifty years after his death, the illness that killed him is commonly referred to as "Lou Gehrig's Disease."

THE GREAT CENTER FIELDERS

With both Ruth and Gehrig gone, the Yankees pinned their hopes on a dynamic young center fielder named Joe DiMaggio, a player who could hit homers and still have a high batting average. DiMaggio twice topped the American League in home runs—with forty-six in 1937 and thirty-nine in 1948—and won AL batting titles in 1939 and 1940. But DiMaggio is best known for what he did in 1941, a year in which he didn't win any home-run or batting championships. It was the year Boston Red Sox slugger Ted Williams became the last hitter to average .400 in a season, but it is still best known as the season Joe DiMaggio recorded at least one base hit in fifty-six consecutive games. No one else has had a batting streak of more than forty-four games. Of all the records set by Yankee players, Joe DiMaggio's fifty-six-game streak may be the most remarkable.

"The 1941 streak was an unbelievable thing—day after day after day," said Yankee shortstop Phil Rizzuto. "I

Like Mantle, Dave Winfield was a powerful hitter.

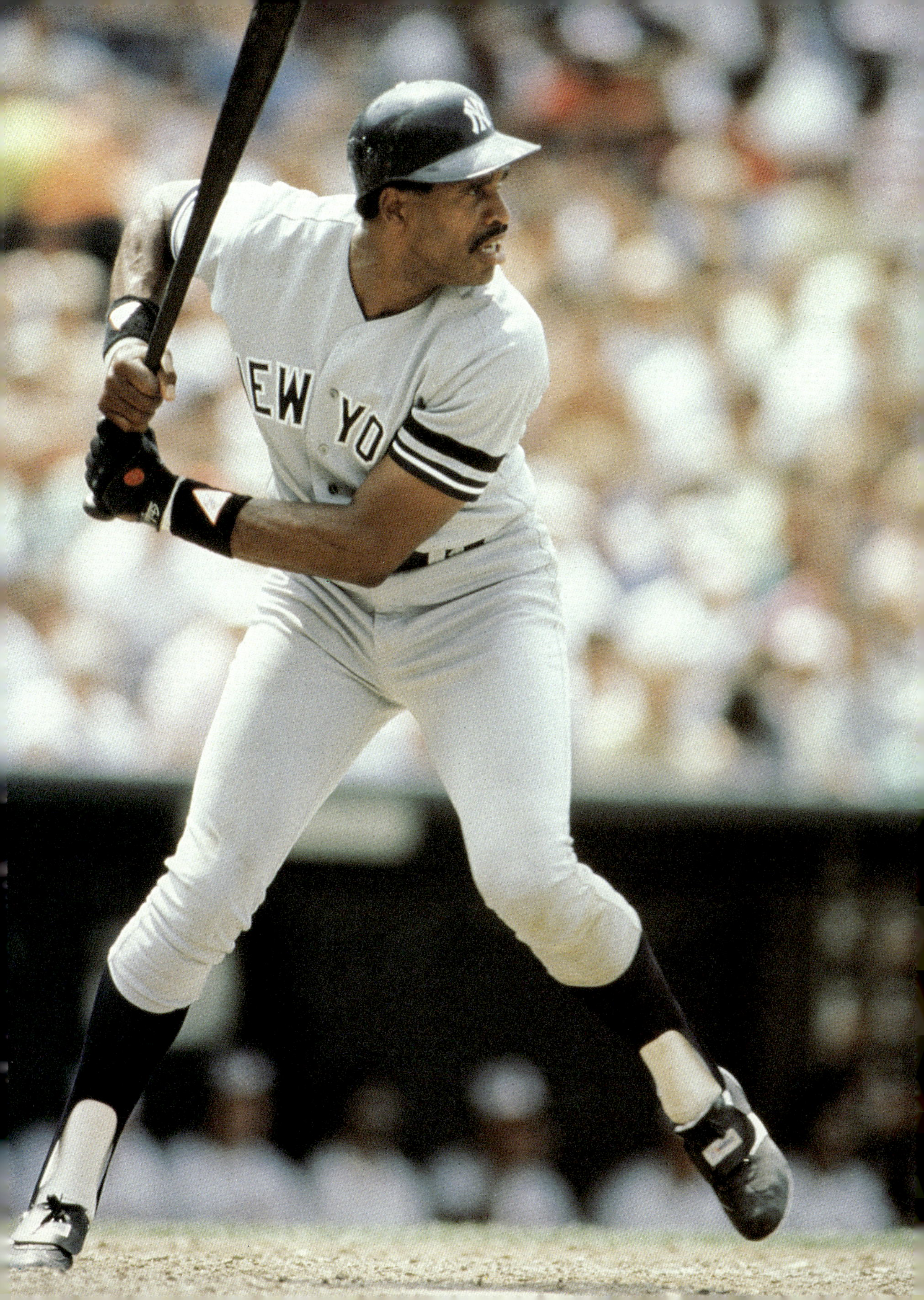

In his first full season as skipper, Casey Stengal led the Yankees to the World Series championship.

don't think he got a soft hit the entire fifty-six games. There were so many great games in the streak. He got up to forty or forty-five, and you really couldn't see any difference in him. He just acted the same every day."

Success didn't affect Joe DiMaggio; he seemed the same no matter what. "People didn't see DiMaggio like I did," said Yankee pitcher Bill Dickey. "He just was never a guy who could let down in front of strangers. He was a guy who knew he was the greatest baseball player in America, and he was proud of it. He knew what the press and the fans and the kids expected of him, and he was always trying to live up to that image. That's why he couldn't be silly in public like I could, or ever be caught without his shirt buttoned or his shoes shined. He felt that obligation to the Yankees and to the public."

Joe DiMaggio gave the Yankees sixteen years of exemplary service. During his years in New York, the team won eleven pennants and ten World Series titles. DiMaggio, who slammed 361 homers in his career, was named the American League's Most Valuable Player three times—in 1939, 1941, and 1947. Despite his success, some of DiMaggio's teammates felt he didn't receive the credit he deserved. "I think DiMaggio was underestimated as a player," said Bill Dickey. "He did things so easily people didn't realize how good he was. DiMaggio would hit a home run, but nobody would get excited. He could do so many things to keep the other team from beating you."

When DiMaggio quit after the 1951 season, Yankee fans wondered where the team would find someone to replace him. As it turned out, the Yankees didn't have to look very far—only to right field, where a twenty-year-old named Mickey Mantle was playing during

Catcher Elston Howard starred for the Yanks in the 1950s.

The one and only, Mickey Mantle

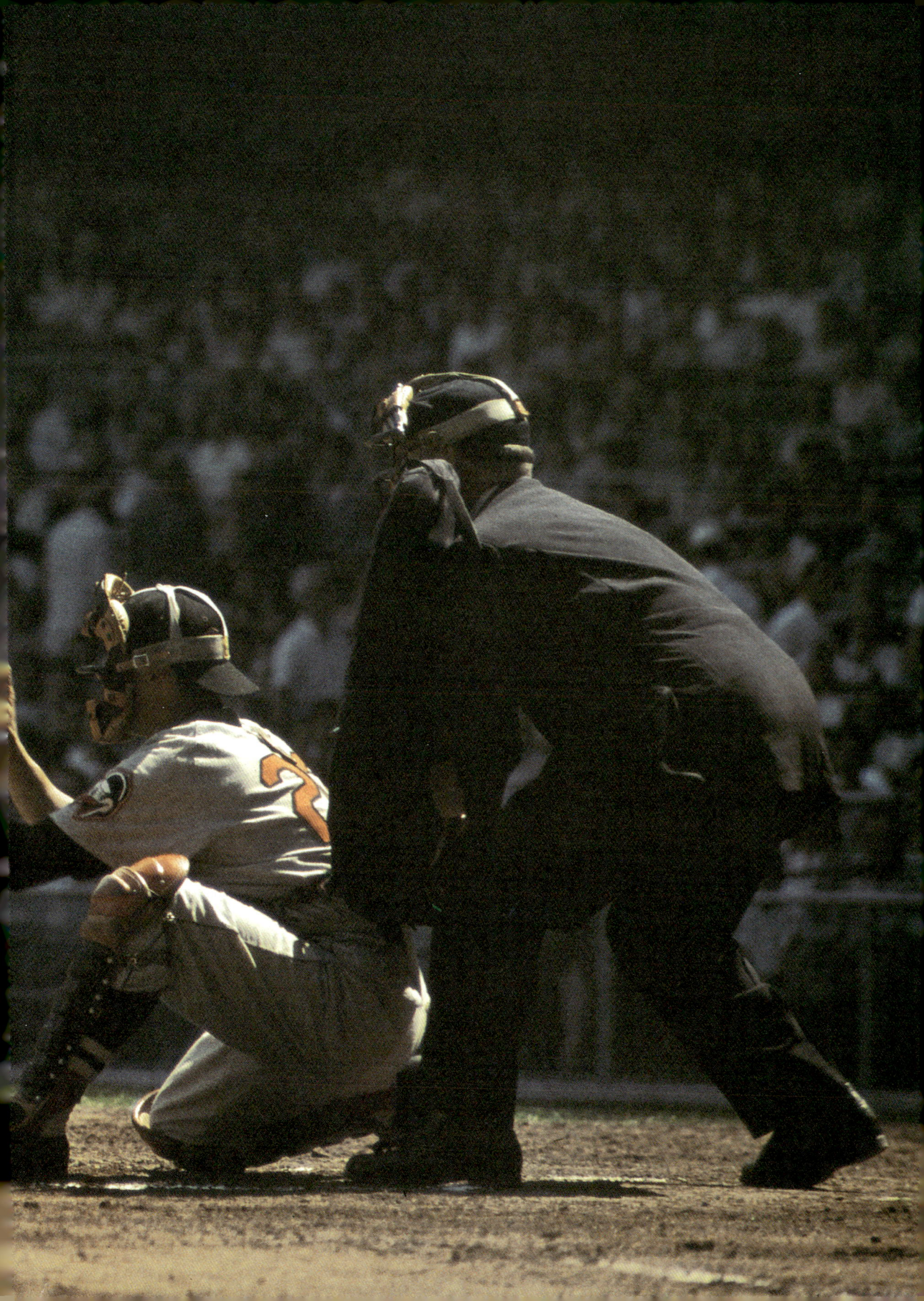

1 9 5 1

The great and long career of "The Yankee Clipper", Joe Dimaggio (right), came to an end.

DiMaggio's final season in New York. Mantle, who had grown up in Oklahoma, was unlike previous Yankee sluggers. A switch-hitter, he could launch mammoth home runs either right- or left-handed.

Mantle had made an immediate impression on Yankee coaches the first time he took batting practice. Although he was only eighteen years old at the time, he hit several balls that traveled more than five hundred feet. Yankee manager Casey Stengel could hardly believe his eyes. "Tell ya how it is," Stengel said. "There are some who say he hits with more power right-handed, and there's others who say he hits with more power left-handed. They can't make up their minds. Now, wouldn't you say that was amazing? Personally, I hope they never find out."

Mantle, however, wasn't a star at first. He struggled in the minor leagues for a couple of seasons until he finally found his hitting stroke and was called up to the majors. There he joined a Yankee team that had such stars as pitchers Whitey Ford and Ralph Terry, shortstop Phil Rizzuto, second baseman Bobby Richardson, and catcher Yogi Berra. Rizzuto had been voted American League MVP in 1950, and Berra was the AL's Most Valuable Player three times—in 1951, 1954, and 1955. By 1956, though, Mickey Mantle was New York's top player. In fact, he was probably the best player in all of baseball that year. Mantle won the Triple Crown in the American League in 1956 by leading the league in home runs (fifty-two), runs batted in (130), and batting average (.353). Not surprisingly, Mantle was voted the American League MVP.

Behind the fine play of Mickey Mantle the Yankees won their fifth consecutive World Championship.

Unfortunately for Mantle, who also won the league MVP honor in 1957 and 1962, his career was hampered by injuries, particularly to his knees. Once one of the fastest players in the game, Mantle started to run as if he were crippled. He still managed to retain some of his speed, but the pain took its toll. Mantle, though, played no matter how much his body ached. During the 1961 World Series, in which the Yankees played the Cincinnati Reds, Mantle was in the lineup despite a large infection in his hip. The infection had developed while Mantle was hospitalized with a bad virus. The illness had come in a season when both Mantle and teammate Roger Maris were on pace to break Babe Ruth's single-season home-run record. Maris went on to break the record; Mantle went on to the hospital, because of his ailment. He still managed to hit fifty-four home runs, second only to Maris's sixty-one.

After missing the first two games of the series, Mantle played in games three and four, helping the Yankees to

A star for today, Don Mattingly.

two victories and a 3–1 lead in the series. But Mantle had to come out of the fourth game after hitting a single; the pain from the open wound on his hip was just too much. "It made me sick to look at the hole in his hip," said New York catcher Elston Howard. "It makes me sick to think about it. Nobody else would have played. Nobody. But Mickey isn't like normal people."

Despite Mantle's injury, the Yankees wound up winning the 1961 World Series in five games. A year later Mickey Mantle endured another series of injuries, but somehow managed to win league MVP honors and lead the team to another World Series triumph, this time over the San Francisco Giants. However, it would be the last World Series victory for the New York team for fifteen years. The Yankees, behind the aging Mantle, won pennants in 1963 and 1964, but the team, and its star, soon fell off. By the late 1960s, the Yankees were no longer even pennant contenders. Mickey Mantle's body finally gave out, and he retired with 536 home runs, which remains the eighth-highest total in major-league history. There is no telling what Mantle might have achieved had he been healthy most of his career. As Casey Stengel said of Mantle, "He's the only man I ever saw who was a cripple and could outdo the world."

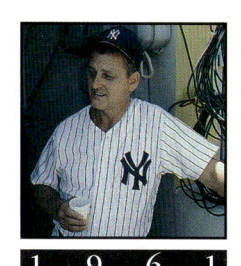

Roger Maris' 61st home run broke Babe Ruth's single season home run record.

THE MODERN YANKS: JACKSON AND MATTINGLY

The Yankees weren't outdoing many American League teams during the late 1960s and early 1970s. The club changed players, coaches, and managers, and nothing worked. Then, in 1972, the Yankees had an

24   *Left to right: Chris Chambliss, Sparky Lyle, Graig Nettles, Dave Righetti.*

ownership change that would bring about a brief reversal of the franchise's fortunes. George Steinbrenner bought the team and announced he was determined to build it into a champion, regardless of what it cost. Steinbrenner then proceeded to purchase such great talents as pitcher Jim "Catfish" Hunter and slugging outfielder Reggie Jackson. These players were combined with Yankee stars such as catcher Thurman Munson, third baseman Graig Nettles, first baseman Chris Chambliss, and relief pitcher Sparky Lyle to produce a rising power in the American League.

In 1976 the Yankees won the pennant for the first time in twelve years, but were swept four games to none by the Cincinnati Reds in the World Series. A year later, though, nothing could stop the Yankees. They won the American League pennant and then took a three-games-to-two lead against the Los Angeles Dodgers in the World Series. Then Reggie Jackson took over. Jackson, who had already slammed two homers in the series, hit homers in his first two at bats of game six. When he came to the plate for the third time, the Yankee fans were on their feet screaming "REG-GIE, REG-GIE, REG-GIE."

"I thought if I got a decent pitch, I could hit another one out," Jackson said. "Anyway, at that point, I couldn't lose. All I had to do was show up at the plate. They were going to cheer me even if I struck out. So the last one [at bat] was strictly dreamland." The last one was also a nightmare for the Dodgers, as Jackson hammered Charlie Hough's knuckleball over the center-field fence for his third home run of the game and fifth of the series. Only Babe Ruth had hit three homers in a World Series game; Jackson also set a record for most home runs in a series.

Don Gullett became the first free agent signed by the Yankees in the re-entry draft.

Thurman Munson (pages 26–27).

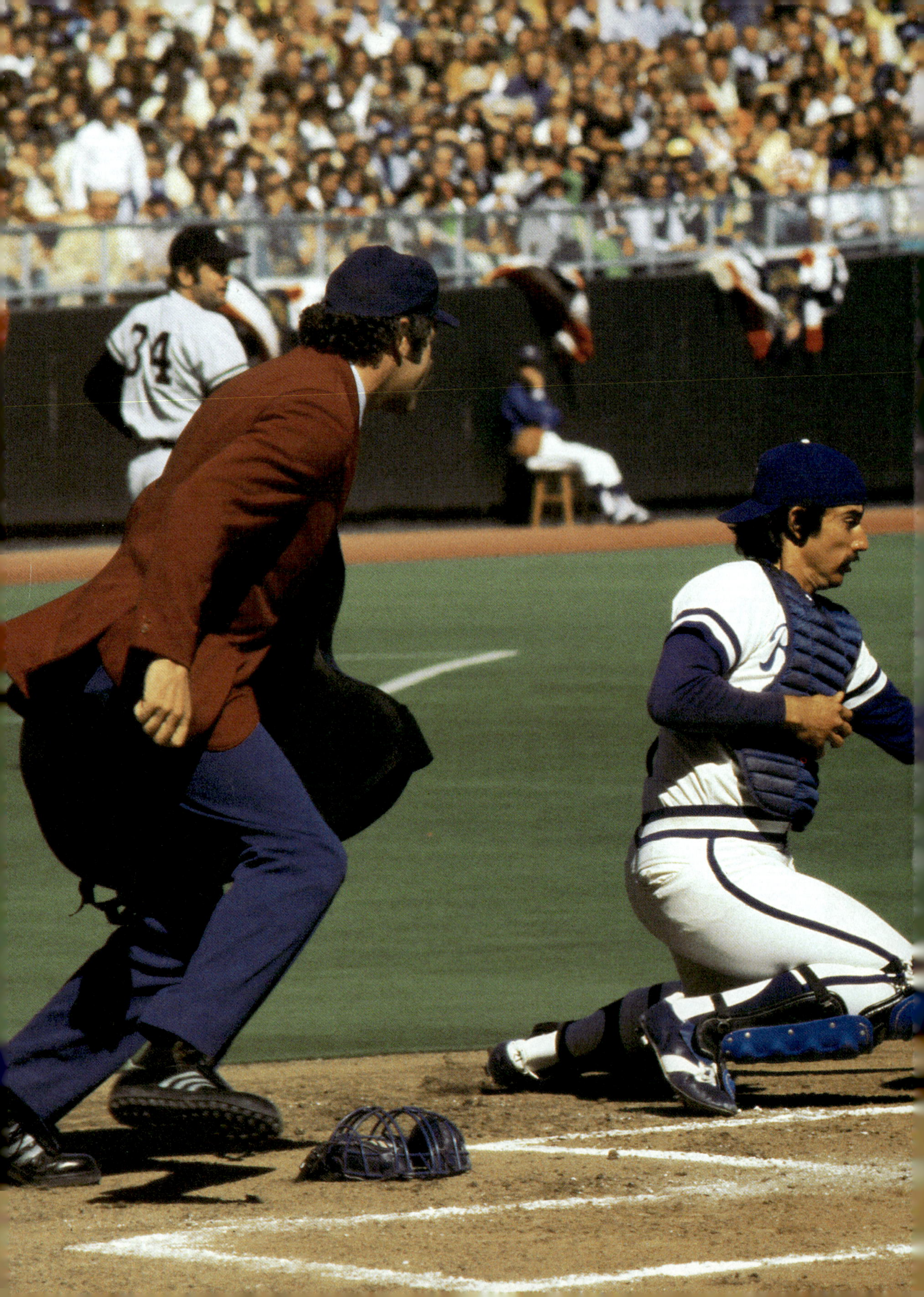

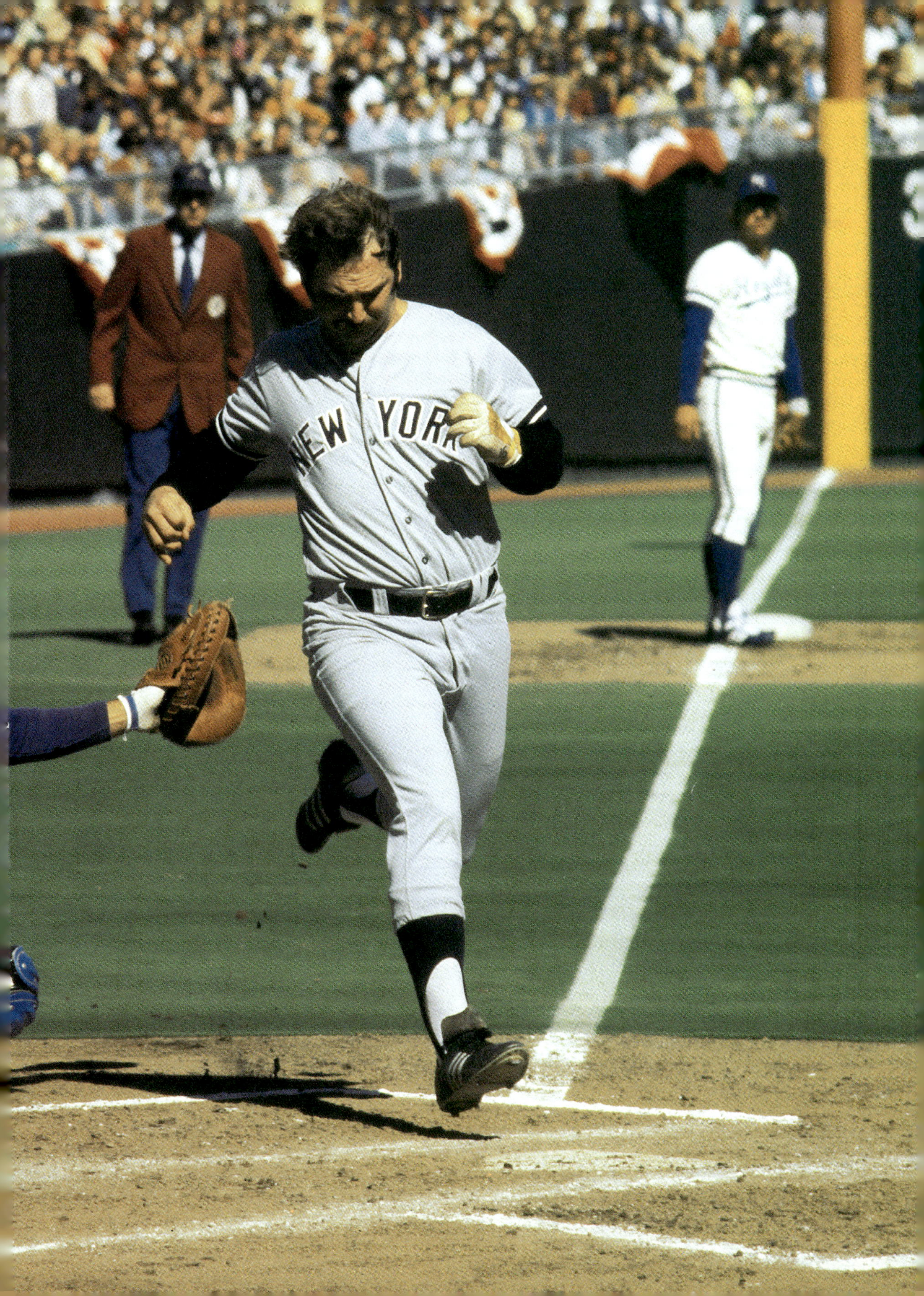
NEW YORK

On August 4, the Yankees celebrated Phil Rizzuto Day and retired his uniform number, 10.

Thanks to Jackson's power, the Yankees won the game and the series.

Jackson and the Yankees won another World Series title in 1978, beating the Dodgers again. Pitcher Ron Guidry won the American League's Cy Young Award, and shortstop Bucky Dent was the Most Valuable Player in the World Series. The Yankees also won the East Division of the American League in both 1980 and 1981, and were AL pennant winners in 1981. But the success ended; the team's stars had gotten old, and George Steinbrenner wasn't having too much luck replacing them with high-priced free agents. Still, both Dave Winfield and Rickey Henderson, a pair of outfielders, had several solid seasons for the club. And no Yankee was more consistent during the 1980s than first baseman Don Mattingly, who was the American League's Most Valuable Player in 1985 and who also won the league batting title in 1984.

Mattingly brings an intense attitude to the ballpark every game. "Check Donnie's eyes during a game," said former Yankee pitcher Bob Tewksbury. "They're right out of a horror movie. He yells at opposing players. He paces in the dugout. I've never seen anyone compete with that kind of passion." Mattingly's intensity comes naturally. "I don't actually dislike any opposing players, but I hate them when I play against them," Mattingly said. "Especially pitchers. I'm competing with them, every at bat, 162 games a season. You have to hate the guy. You have to get your mind into a sort of rage. I try to think of all the things the guy has done to irk me over the years. Fortunately, I seldom forget things."

Unfortunately for Mattingly, one of baseball's bright stars, the Yankees have forgotten how to be champions.

1 9 9 0

Up-and-coming star Roberto Kelly (left) slides in safely against Mike Heath of Detroit.

New York is the only team in the American League East Division besides Cleveland not to have won a title in the last eight years. Mattingly, who is considered one of the top clutch players in the game, has never really been involved in a pennant race. "Until you see Don Mattingly in a pennant race, you have not seen the real Don Mattingly," said former New York third baseman Mike Pagliarulo, one of Mattingly's best friends. "He doesn't care about stats. He wants to win."

So do the Yankees, but they have a long rebuilding process in front of them. Mattingly, outfielders Roberto Kelly and Oscar Azocar, shortstop Alvaro Espinoza, second baseman Steve Sax, and relief pitcher Dave Righetti represent a foundation for the future, but the team desperately needs more pitching and more power.

Shortstop Alvaro Espinoza.

Outfielder Oscar Azocar.

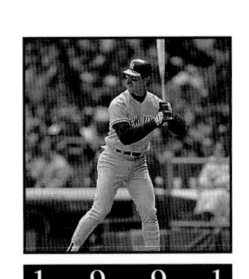

Despite the loss of Dave Righetti, the Yankees and Don Mattingly were much improved.

The team got some of this needed power during the 1990 season when first baseman Kevin Maas was called up from the minor leagues to replace the injured Don Mattingly. Maas immediately began launching mammoth home runs. During his first two months in the majors, Maas averaged one homer every nine at bats. His performance shocked Yankee fans, who weren't used to quality players emerging from New York's farm system. "It's not like I came out of nowhere," Maas protested. "I hit some homers in the minors." The young player's accomplishments in the major leagues impressed New York officials so much, they began talking about moving Mattingly to the outfield to make room for Maas.

Maas also impressed the New York fans, some of whom compared him with legendary Yankee stars of the past. Maas was called the next Babe Ruth, or Lou Gehrig, or Joe DiMaggio, or Mickey Mantle, or Reggie Jackson. These were the players who led the team during its glory days, which lasted more than forty years. Maas, Mattingly, and Company hope to recapture those good times.